IS IT ROSH HASHANAH YET?

CHRIS BARASH

Pictures by
ALESSANDRA
PSACHAROPULO

ALBERT WHITMAN & COMPANY
CHICAGO, ILLINOIS

When summer's almost over
but we feel the bright sun's heat

And the garden still has veggies
that our family loves to eat...

Rosh Hashanah is on its way.

When we take a Sunday car ride to the orchard that's nearby

And pick fruit for Daddy's applesauce, and more to bake a pie...

Rosh Hashanah is on its way.

When Mom buys pomegranates
(a fruit I've never tried!)

And we hope to do a *mitzvah* for each of the seeds inside...

Rosh Hashanah is on its way.

When we cut out paper apples, all yellow, red, and green
And make cards for all our family—the best they've ever seen!

HAPPY
NEW
YEAR!

L'Shanah
Tovah!

Rosh Hashanah is on its way.

When Nana comes to visit and brings honey, sticky-sweet
To eat with crunchy apples for our favorite New Year treat...

Rosh Hashanah is on its way.

When the month of Elul's ending and Tishrei's coming fast
And from the shofar blower we hear the ram's horn blast...

Rosh Hashanah is on its way.

When people smile and say hello and "*Shanah Tovah*" too
And what they're really saying is "a good New Year to you!"

Rosh Hashanah is on its way.

When so many people visit that there's no place left to sit

And our living room is crowded, but no one cares a bit...

When Nana's lit the candles and blessings have been said

And Mom calls, "Let's eat this brisket before it's time for bed!"

Rosh Hashanah is here!

Celebrate throughout the year with other books in this series!

Is It Purim Yet?   Is It Passover Yet?   Is It Sukkot Yet?   Is It Hanukkah Yet?

For CL, who likes books with lots of pictures—CB
To Tommaso—AP

Library of Congress Cataloging-in-Publication data
is on file with the publisher.

Text copyright © 2018 by Chris Barash
Pictures copyright © 2018 by Alessandra Psacharopulo
First published in the United States of America in 2018 by Albert Whitman & Company
ISBN 978-0-8075-3396-3

Printed in China
10 9 8 7 6 5 4 3 2 1 LP 22 21 20 19 18

Design by Jordan Kost and Morgan Beck

For more information about Albert Whitman & Company,
visit our website at www.albertwhitman.com.